THE BINDER OF

DOOM

BRUTE-CAKE

by Troy Cummings

BRANCHES

SCHOLASTIC INC.

TABLE OF CONTENTS

To Harvey. I hope to one day write stories as funny as yours.

Copyright © 2019 by Troy Cummings

All rights reserved. Published by Scholastic Inc., *Publishers since 1920*. SCHOLASTIC, BRANCHES, and associated logos are trademarks and/or registered trademarks of Scholastic Inc.

The publisher does not have any control over and does not assume any responsibility for author or third-party websites or their content.

No part of this publication may be reproduced, stored in a retrieval system, or transmitted in any form or by any means, electronic, mechanical, photocopying, recording, or otherwise, without written permission of the publisher. For information regarding permission, write to Scholastic Inc., Attention: Permissions Department, 557 Broadway, New York, NY 10012.

This book is a work of fiction. Names, characters, places, and incidents are either the product of the author's imagination or are used fictitiously, and any resemblance to actual persons, living or dead, business establishments, events, or locales is entirely coincidental.

Library of Congress Cataloging-in-Publication Data

Names: Cummings, Troy, author.

Title: Brute-cake / by Troy Cummings.

Description: First edition. | New York, NY : Branches/Scholastic Inc., 2019. | Series: The binder of doom ; 1 |

Summary: It has been several months since monsters last plagued the town of Stermont, and frankly Alexander Bopp (leader of the Super Secret Monster Patrol) is bored, and misses his friends Rip (immersed in video games) and Nikki (soccer camp), so when his father signs him up for a summer maker program at the library he is happy to go--but soon he starts finding weird old-timey objects, and monster trading cards, and it starts to look like maybe monsters are back in Stermont.

Identifiers: LCCN 2018035381| ISBN 9781338314663 (pbk.) | ISBN 9781338314670 (hardcover)

Subjects: LCSH: Monsters – Juvenile fiction. | Makerspaces in libraries – Juvenile fiction. | Public libraries – Juvenile fiction. | Best friends – Juvenile fiction. | Horror tales. | CYAC: Monsters – Fiction. | Makerspaces – Fiction. | Libraries – Fiction. | Best friends – Fiction. | Friendship – Fiction. | Horror stories. | LCGFT: Horror fiction.

Classification: LCC PZ7.C91494 Br 2019 | DDC 813.6 [Fic] – dc23 LC record available at https://catalog.loc.gov/2018035381

10 9 8 7 6 5 4 3   19 20 21 22 23

Printed in China   62

First edition, May 2019

Edited by Katie Carella

Book design by Troy Cummings and Sarah Dvojack

CHAPTER 1

BACK TO NORMAL

Alexander Bopp was having a pretty weird day.

Actually, not just a pretty weird day — the *most* weird day. And he was an expert on weird days.

Today was weirder than:

1. the day he moved to an odd little town called Stermont

2. the day he was first attacked by a monster

3. the many, many days he battled monsters.

Today was weirder than all of those days, because today was perfectly, totally, absolutely normal. Stermont was safe. The monsters were gone. The school year had just ended.

Alexander watched his friends and teachers pack up and go their separate ways. Then he cleaned out his desk and shuffled out of Stermont Elementary.

Everything is just so weird! Alexander thought as he walked home.

Weirdest of all, he and his two best friends — Rip and Nikki — had drifted apart.

Together, they were the members of a club sworn to protect Stermont from monsters.

SUPER SECRET MONSTER PATROL

MEMBERS ▷	RIP	NIKKI	ALEXANDER
The good old days	Tough on monsters (and some kids). Loyal to Alexander.	Smart and fast. Always had her friends' backs.	Creative and full of energy. Leader of the S.S.M.P.
The past few months	With no monsters to fight, Rip spent all his time playing video games.	Nikki joined the soccer team and spent all her time on the field.	 Homework. Bedtime. Repeat.
Now	Collecting gems on level 9-2 (ice world). 	Soccer camp! 	Lonely. 

The S.S.M.P. used to meet every day. Then they met once a week. And then, when several months had passed with no monster attacks, they stopped meeting altogether. Alexander wondered if he would see his friends at all this summer.

He sighed as he walked into his house.

"Hey, kiddo!" his dad sang out. "How was your last day of school?"

Alexander wanted to say, "I miss fighting monsters with my friends, Dad. I kinda sorta wish a monster would attack *right now*, so the Super Secret Monster Patrol could get back together."

4

But he couldn't say those things. Grown-ups didn't know about monsters. They couldn't see them. So Alexander just grumbled, shrugged, and plopped into his beanbag.

"Easy there, Mr. Grumpy — I've got fantastic news!" said Alexander's dad. "I signed you up for a whole summer of crazy-cool activities with the S.S.M.P.!"

Alexander fell off his beanbag. He suddenly couldn't wait for summer to get started.

CHAPTER 2

MS. SPRINKLES

The next morning, Alexander's thoughts swirled around like the cereal in his bowl.

"Dad?" he finally asked. "How long have you known about the S.S.M.P.?"

"Oh, I dunno," said his dad, between bites of toast. "A few days, I guess. Ever since a nice businessman gave me this flyer."

Stermont Summer Maker Program!

SUMMER CAMP at the STERMONT PUBLIC LIBRARY!

Join Ms. Sprinkles for 12 weeks of:

 ART! GAMES! MUSIC! MAKER SPACE!

 PUPPETRY! BRICK BUILDING! CHESS!

"Oh," said Alexander. He swallowed the last soggy lump of cereal. "The Stermont Summer Maker Program . . . Summer camp at the library."

"It'll be swell!" said his dad. "You'll do maker stuff all day while I'm doing dentist stuff. And look — they've got chess!"

Alexander smiled. "Sounds good, Dad."

After breakfast, Alexander biked downtown — slowly. *I'm in no hurry to get to* this *S.S.M.P.*, he thought. *Especially without Rip and Nikki.*

SCREECH! He skidded to a stop near the library. There was a new billboard across the street.

That's odd, Alexander thought. *Why would anyone buy a bike like that?*

He parked his bike and headed into the library.

A woman sat at the front desk, writing on a clipboard. She had frizzy brown hair that went in all directions. Alexander read the nameplate on the desk.

"Welcome!" she said. "Are you here for the summer program?"

"Um, yes — I'm Alexander Bopp."

"Wonderful!" she said. "I'm Ms. Sprinkles."

She led Alexander upstairs.

The second story of the library felt like a magic forest. It was full of cozy nooks that looked like trees, and a little stage that looked like a waterfall. A few kids were lounging on lily-pad cushions, reading. Windows on all sides filled the forest with sunlight.

Alexander walked over to the windows.

"I can see the whole town from up here!" he said.

"Yes! Yes!" said Ms. Sprinkles. "In fact — that view is part of our first activity!"

She stood on the stage and called out, in a singsong voice, "Maker-bees, buzz on over!"

The lily-pad kids made their way to the stage.

They looked nice enough, but none of them were Rip or Nikki.

Ms. Sprinkles gave everyone a shiny new binder.

"This summer, you'll fill your binders with amazing creations," she said, "starting with a map of downtown Stermont."

The kids got to work.

SNAP! Alexander put his map in his binder.

"You're finished already?" asked Ms. Sprinkles.

"Yep!" said Alexander. "I like making maps." *And monster diagrams . . . and super-secret battle plans,* he thought.

"Nice work! You even got the hedge maze next door," she said. "Now you can get a jump on our next activity — games!"

Ms. Sprinkles pointed Alexander to a bookcase that looked like a castle.

Alexander found a chess book. Someone had left a bookmark in the last chapter.

It looked like some sort of trading card — with a monster on it!

Alexander felt his skin prickle as he touched the card.

DRILL-PICKLE

LEVEL 3

Tunneling terror from the salty, briny deep.

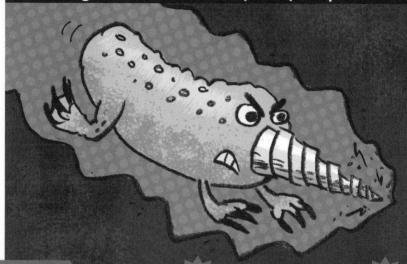

ATTACKS **DRILL-DIVE!** 25 **CLAW-SCRABBLE!** 15

HABITAT

Jars at the bottom of the sea.

DIET

Salt and vinegar.

TYPE

FOOD

THINGY

The drill-pickle can burrow through dirt, clay, or solid stone.

FLYING SPACE-CARS

Alexander stared at the card. The monster's angry eyes seemed to stare back. Then, just as he tucked the card into his binder, he felt a tap on his shoulder.

He gasped.

"Hello, Salamander," said a girl's voice behind him.

Salamander was Alexander's nickname. And only one girl called him that. He turned to see one of his best friends in the world, Nikki Hubbard.

"Nikki!" Alexander shouted. "I thought you'd be at soccer camp!"

Nikki gave Alexander a hug. "The fields are flooded," she said. "A big water pipe broke or something. So I signed up for the Stermont Summer Maker Program."

Alexander laughed. "Kind of weird how we're both in a club called S.S.M.P. again."

"But *this* club doesn't have anything to do with monsters," said Nikki.

"Well, there is *one* monster," Alexander whispered. "You!"

Nikki was secretly a good monster, called a jampire.

Fangs!

Hates sunlight.

Sees in the dark.

Eats red, juicy stuff, like strawberries with ketchup.

THUNK! Ms. Sprinkles set a bin of toy bricks on the worktable. "Gather round!" she announced. "It's time for our morning maker challenge!"

She wrote on the whiteboard:

Design a car
from the year
3000.

The campers spent the rest of the morning building futuristic cars.

Except for Alexander. He built something else.

"Uh, Salamander," said Nikki. "That's one weird-looking car."

"It's not a car," said Alexander.

"It's a DRILL-PICKLE!"

"Huh?" said Nikki.

"Don't panic," Alexander whispered. "But look what I found." He showed her the monster card.

"Whoa!" whispered Nikki. "It looks like you've stumbled upon . . ."

Alexander leaned in closer.

". . . a silly trading-card game!" Nikki laughed.

"What?! NO!" Alexander said, a little too loudly. His brick monster slipped from his hands.

The other kids looked up from their space-cars.

Ms. Sprinkles smiled. "When kids get wiggly, it's time for a break," she said. "Let's head to lunch!"

The campers followed Ms. Sprinkles outside. They sat around a fountain to eat.

Alexander took another peek at the monster card.

"Oh, Salamander," said Nikki, chomping a raspberry. "I'm sure that card's just from some goofy game."

Alexander took a whale-sized bite of his sandwich. "NUH-UH!" he said, with a mouthful of peanut butter. "MRFF-MWRFF-MURM the monsters are back!"

NOTE OF DOOM

After lunch, Ms. Sprinkles led the campers to the music closet. She opened the door and frowned.

"That's odd!" she said. "How did *this* get in here?"

She carried out an old-timey record player.

"My great-grandpa has one of those," said May.

"Let's give it a whirl!" said Ms. Sprinkles.

She cranked the record player. The record spun, and a few dried crumbs flew off.

Alexander picked one up. *Bread crumbs?* he wondered.

Scratchy tuba music filled the library.

"All right, maker-bees," Ms. Sprinkles said. "The rest of your first day is free time. Go make something!"

Everyone spread out. The other kids pulled Nikki away for more brick building.

Alexander sighed and climbed into a nook. He cracked open his chess book.

Ms. Sprinkles popped her head into Alexander's tree. "I see you're reading about the mighty pawn."

"'Mighty?!'" said Alexander. "Pawns are the smallest piece on the board!"

Ms. Sprinkles smiled. "Pawns may be small, but they're smart. They know how to block the powerful pieces. And set traps. And work as a team."

Just like Rip, Nikki, and me in the old S.S.M.P., thought Alexander.

"Let's play a game or two, and you'll see how awesome pawns are," said Ms. Sprinkles. "Just don't take it personally when I CRUSH YOU!"

Alexander laughed. She had said the last part in a fake pro-wrestling voice.

By the end of the afternoon, Alexander had lost to Ms. Sprinkles five times in a row. Finally, it was time to leave.

Alexander found Nikki over by the cubbies.

"There you are!" he said.

"Salamander!" she said. "I made something for you." She tossed Alexander a brick sculpture of a square-headed kid.

"It's Rip!" said Alexander. "I'd recognize that blockhead anywhere."

"I kind of miss him," said Nikki.

"Me too," said Alexander. "We should totally —"

Alexander froze. There was a bright red envelope in his cubby. Someone had drawn a skull on it and had written a single word.

DEAD END

Alexander felt his heart race as he picked up the envelope.

"Weird," said Nikki. "You got a letter — in your library cubby?"

"Let's go read it outside," Alexander whispered.

They ran out to the bike rack.

Alexander tore open the envelope. There was a note inside.

TO ALEXANDER BOPP:
I AM WAITING FOR YOU
BEHIND THE HOUSE
NEXT TO THE LIBRARY.
FIND ME HERE
AND MEET YOUR
DOOOOOM!!!
SINCERELY:
YOUR WORST NIGHTMARE
P.S. MWA-HA-HAAA!!

"Yikes!" said Nikki as Alexander put the note in his binder. "That's a mean note."

"It *must* be from a monster!" he said.

Nikki twiddled her hoodie strings. "But the monsters are gone — we took down every last one."

"We should make sure," said Alexander.

Nikki nodded.

They headed to the house next door.

"Looks like nobody's home," said Nikki.

"But the note says 'behind the house,'" said
Alexander. "Let's peek in the backyard."

Alexander and Nikki tiptoed through
a grove of dead trees until they
reached a tall gate.

"The Brambles . . ."
Nikki read. "What's that?"

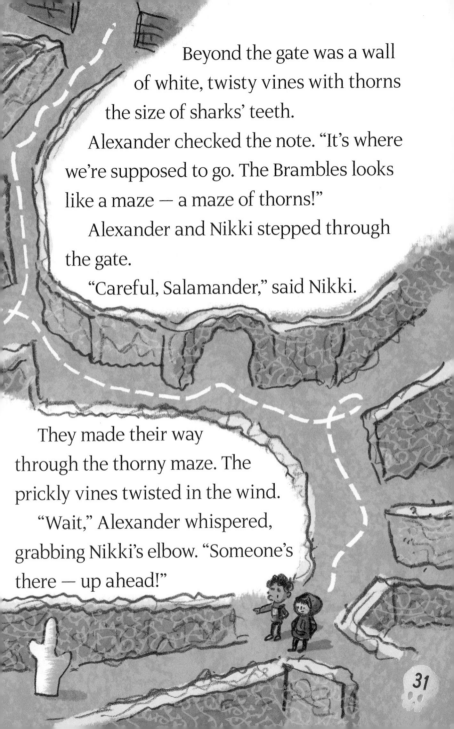

Beyond the gate was a wall of white, twisty vines with thorns the size of sharks' teeth.

Alexander checked the note. "It's where we're supposed to go. The Brambles looks like a maze — a maze of thorns!"

Alexander and Nikki stepped through the gate.

"Careful, Salamander," said Nikki.

They made their way through the thorny maze. The prickly vines twisted in the wind.

"Wait," Alexander whispered, grabbing Nikki's elbow. "Someone's there — up ahead!"

"That's a statue," said Nikki.

"Oh, right," said Alexander. "I knew that."

They walked up to the statue. It was shiny and white, and sort of looked like a cactus.

CLONK-CLONK-CLONK! Alexander knocked on the statue. It was rock solid.

"Let's keep moving," said Nikki.

They passed several more strange white statues.

Suddenly, something dashed out from the wall of prickly vines.

"Ack!" Alexander jumped back, catching his arm on a thorn. "Ow!"

"That was just a squirrel, Salamander!" said Nikki. She untangled Alexander's ripped sleeve.

"MRUUUGGHH!!!" A low moan came from deeper in the maze.

Nikki's eyes widened. "Squirrels don't make *that* sound!"

"Let's see what it is," said Alexander.

They ran toward the sound and soon reached a dead end. They saw another white statue. This one was shaped like a spider.

"MRUUUGGHH!!!"

"The moans are coming from *that*!" said Nikki.

Alexander took a step toward the spider. "Here I am! I got your note!" he shouted.

The statue began to shake. So did Alexander. And then —

"RAAAH!!" A square-headed figure leapfrogged over the statue, straight for Alexander.

THE ACTION HERO

"**G**otcha, weenie!" the square-headed figure yelled as he tackled Alexander.

It was Alexander's other best friend in the world, Rip Bonkowski. "My note worked! You totally thought I was a monster!"

Nikki slugged Rip on the arm. "You *are* a monster!"

"Takes one to know one!" said Rip.

Alexander smiled as he watched Nikki and Rip argue.

"It's been forever since we've all hung out," said Alexander. "You should've left us a mystery note months ago, Rip!"

"I've been busy," Rip said. "But I made you something! Here, check out my new comic!" He pulled a wadded-up page from his pocket.

THE AWESOME ADVENTURES OF
THE AMAAAAAA

Once there was a handsome athlete with great eyebrows and killer dance moves. (Rip.) Everyone in Stermont agreed that he rocked.

But then — BLAMMO! — a million monsters attacked! Most people were scared. Not Rip!

STEP ASIDE, WEENIES!

AAZING RIP!

In addition to being awesome, Rip had a dangerous secret. Long ago, he ate monster candy. Now whenever he eats sweets, Rip transforms into the <u>knuckle-fisted punch-smasher</u>!

RAWWRR!!!

RIP FACT! Rip carries a pocketful of monster ants, who become GI-NORM-ANTS when they eat sugar.

Anyway, Monster-Rip defeated all the monsters in town.*

POW!

Then Rip vowed to never become a monster again. Instead, he became a big-shot cartoonist.

THE END!

*With help from his assistants:
Alexander: A regular boy.   Nikki: A jampire girl.

 Be careful, Rip!

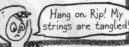 Hang on, Rip! My strings are tangled!

"Epic comic, huh?" said Rip.

"Yeah." Alexander laughed. "You're a real hero."

"Hey, what's up with the last part of your comic — where you promise never to turn into a monster again?" asked Nikki.

"Eh. Monster-Rip has been getting Me-Rip into trouble. Of course, my mom doesn't know I'm a monster, but she keeps saying sweets make me too hyper." He kicked the dirt. "Besides, the bad monsters are all gone so I don't really *need* my powers anymore."

"What if the monsters are *not* all gone?" Alexander asked. "I found a strange card —"

"Face it, Salamander," Nikki interrupted. "Our monster-fighting days are behind us. Now we just do regular-kid stuff, like play soccer."

"And video games!" added Rip. "When we moved to this house, Mom got me a new computer with —"

"You MOVED?" repeated Alexander. He frowned.

"Here?" Nikki asked.

"Yup," said Rip. "Mom got the house super cheap."

"That's great, Rip!" said Nikki.

"It's the coolest, creepiest place ever," Rip said. "That's why I dragged you both here — to invite you to a sleepover. Tomorrow night!"

But Alexander was hardly listening. He felt like he'd been hit by a steamroller.

"I can't believe you *moved* and didn't tell us sooner," said Alexander. "That's giant news! I thought we were your best friends."

"Whoa, Salamander," said Nikki.

"Sheesh," said Rip. "I didn't think it was a big deal."

"Well, it is!" Alexander shouted.

It got quiet, except for the thornbushes twisting in the wind.

Alexander saw Rip and Nikki share a look.

"I need to get home," Alexander said. "I'm not sure if I can make it to your sleepover." He turned and ran.

QUACKING UP

Alexander stormed up the steps to his house, ready to slam the door behind him. But he paused on the welcome mat.

His front door had a new doorknob. Actually, it had an *old* doorknob that looked like a glass jewel.

"Dad?!" he shouted. "Why did you change our doorknob?"

He looked down. There were crumbs on the welcome mat. *Like on Ms. Sprinkles's record player*, he thought.

41

"Is that you, Al?" his dad called from upstairs. "Up here, kiddo!"

Alexander tromped up to his bedroom.

"Surprise!" his dad sang out.

Alexander's backpack hit the floor. So did his jaw.

Duck wallpaper

Duck pillows

Duck curtains

Duck lamp

Duck trash can

Duck bedspread

"My room has been invaded by ducks," he said.

"Not invaded — redecorated!" said his dad, waving a wallpaper brush. "I took the day off to spruce up your room! Snazzy, huh?"

Alexander groaned and fell onto his bed.

His dad sat next to Alexander. "Sorry, kiddo. I thought you'd like the surprise."

"Why does everything have to change? My friends, our club, and now my bedroom?" said Alexander. "I just want things to go back to the way they were!"

"But your new room is more fun than your old room," said Alexander's dad. "You can almost *hear* the ducks quacking!"

Alexander thought about sleeping every night in a room full of quacking ducks.

He buried his head under his pillow.

"Anyhow," said Alexander's dad, "there is just one wall to go. Want to scrape off the old paper?"

"I guess," said Alexander. Ripping something sounded pretty good right about now.

He got up and grabbed a loose corner of the wallpaper. He paused. There was a lump under the paper — flat and rectangular.

VVRRRRRIKK! Alexander tore the wallpaper away. Something fluttered to the floor.

Alexander gasped. *Another monster card! How did this get here?* he thought. *Now I'm definitely going to Rip's sleepover tomorrow. I need to convince him and Nikki the monsters are back!*

He quickly scooped up the card.

FRIGHT KITE

LEVEL 1

Swooping, looping, daredevil dive-bomber.

Key: For zapping and lock-picking!

ATTACKS	STRING-TANGLE!	5	LIGHTNING ZAP!	15

HABITAT	DIET	TYPE
 Thunderstorms.	 Baby clouds.	THINGY UNKNOWN

The fright kite can fly through flat spaces.

RIP'S MOM

It was almost dinnertime the next day when Alexander arrived at Rip's new old house. He crossed the overgrown yard and could see someone moving through the stained-glass window of the front door.

He knocked. **BAM-BAM-BAM!**

CREEEEEAK! The door swung open. Alexander smelled something sweet, like muffins.

"Hello there, Alexander!"

A square-headed woman greeted Alexander with a mop and a bear hug.

"Uh, hi, Ms. Bonkowski!" said Alexander.

"Excuse the mess," she said, kicking a crate of doll heads to one side. "We're still fixing things up."

Alexander stepped inside. Rip's house looked like it had been a really fancy place — a hundred years ago. The carpet was worn down, the windows had cobwebs, and there were boxes piled everywhere.

A shiny figure stood nearby.

Another white statue, thought Alexander. *Like we saw in The Brambles.*

This statue looked like a jungle cat. He reached out to touch one of its fangs.

BAM-BAM-BAM!

Alexander jumped.

Ms. Bonkowski opened the door.

"Hi!" said Nikki, stepping inside and looking around. "You sure have a lot of stuff, Ms. Bonkowski!"

Rip's mom laughed. "I guess we do! But all these old-timey knickknacks came with the house." She tossed her mop aside. "I sent Rip to the Speedy-Mart for groceries. While we wait for him, why don't I give you two a quick tour?"

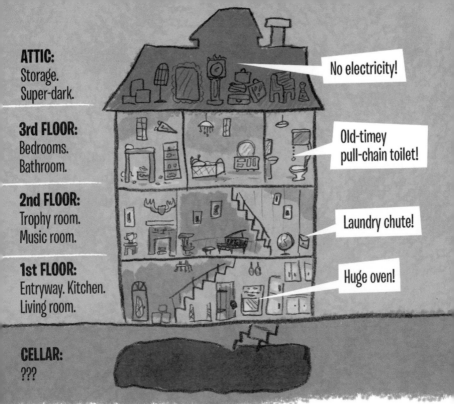

ATTIC:
Storage.
Super-dark.

No electricity!

3rd FLOOR:
Bedrooms.
Bathroom.

Old-timey
pull-chain toilet!

2nd FLOOR:
Trophy room.
Music room.

Laundry chute!

1st FLOOR:
Entryway. Kitchen.
Living room.

Huge oven!

CELLAR:
???

The tour ended in the kitchen. Alexander
pointed to a door with a padlock.

"What's in there?" he asked.

"That's the cellar," said Ms. Bonkowski.
"Unfortunately, we can't unlock the door. The
realtor who sold us the house was super helpful,
but every time I call about that missing key, he
never —"

Ms. Bonkowski stopped in mid-sentence. She was staring at the counter.

"Crumbs! All over my new countertops!" she said. "I've asked Rip to cut back on sweets. He had a cookie in his room last night, and it sounded like a beast was in there trashing the place!"

Alexander shared a look with Nikki.

FLUT-TUT-TUT-TUT-TUT-TUT-TUT!

A rapid-fire fluttering sound came from outside the back door.

MISSED LIST

Alexander looked out the kitchen window and smiled. He ran outside.

FLUT-TUT-TUT-TUT-TUT-TUT-TUT!

Rip biked up the driveway. His back wheel made a fluttering sound.

"Yo, Salamander!" he said, skidding to a halt. "Do you like my super-loud turbo bike? I jammed a card back there so it flaps against the spokes."

"A card?" asked Alexander. "What kind of card?"

"Beats me," said Rip, hopping off his bike. "I found it in my room the day we moved in."

Alexander pulled the card from Rip's bike.

CRABBIT

LEVEL 2

Long ears. Long claws. Short temper.

| ATTACKS | HIPPITY-HOP! | 5 | SNIPPITY-SNAP! | 20 |

HABITAT	DIET	TYPE
 Shredded Easter baskets.	 Carrots, well-chopped.	CRITTER BUG

 A crabbit's long ears allow it to hear the mean things people say about it. That's why it is so snippy.

"THIS is why I came tonight, Rip! I found one of these cards in my bedroom! And in the library," said Alexander. "Hang on — did *you* leave me those cards?"

"Huh? No!" said Rip.

Alexander pocketed the monster card.

"RIPLEY!" shouted Ms. Bonkowski through the kitchen window. "Hurry in with those groceries!"

"Coming, Mom!" said Rip. He ran inside.

Alexander followed him into the kitchen. Nikki was helping Rip's mom clear off the counter, just in time for Rip to dump out the grocery bag.

Milk   **Butter**   **Vanilla**   **Powdered sugar**

"Ripley. Herbert. Bonkowski," said Rip's mom. "Why did you get this stuff? I'm cooking dinner, not icing cupcakes!"

"It was all on your list!" argued Rip. "Look!"

He slapped the grocery list onto the counter.

"Rip, I can see where you erased my list," said Ms. Bonkowski.

"I swear I didn't do it!" Rip yelled. "That's not my handwriting!"

Ms. Bonkowski sighed. "Fine. Order pizza for dinner. My phone's on the table. I'm going upstairs for a bath."

Rip's mom left the kitchen.

1. Pasta shell
MILK
2. Chicken
BUTTER
3. Cheese
VANILLA
4. broccoli
TONS
OF
POWDERED
SUGAR
5. sauce

"Yeesh," said Rip, turning to Alexander and Nikki. "It's super weird that someone messed with Mom's grocery list. You both believe me, right?"

"Eh, whatever," said Nikki. "I'm just glad we're having pizza. I vote for no cheese, double sauce, and extra cherry tomatoes!"

"No! Pepperoni!" said Rip. "Or — Whoa! That's not Mom's phone."

Alexander looked at the telephone on the table. It was the old-fashioned kind, with a dial.

"Did that come with the house?" asked Alexander.

"I've never seen it before," said Rip. "How do you even use it?"

Nikki rolled her eyes. "It's called a rotary phone, silly. Watch." She brushed some crumbs off the phone and dialed the pizza place.

Alexander turned to Rip. "Have you been sneaking sweets?" he asked. "There are crumbs all over your house."

"No way, Salamander," said Rip. "Those crumbs must be from mice or something."

Alexander picked up the grocery list. *Something strange is going on*, he thought.

Nikki hung up the phone.

Then the friends turned back toward the counter and gasped.

The countertop was totally bare. Except for a few crumbs.

CHAPTER 10

DISASTER AREA

"**R**ip's groceries were stolen!" said Alexander, pointing to the countertop.

"There's a bandit! In my house!" Rip yelled.

Nikki frowned. "Rip's mom must have put everything away while we were on the phone."

"That makes more sense," said Rip. "Anyway, let's go play video games while we wait for the pizza."

He led them upstairs to his bedroom. There was a jokey sign on the door:

But when Rip opened the door, Alexander realized it was not a joke.

"Yikes!" said Nikki. "Was your room this much of a disaster when you moved in?"

"What — no!" said Rip. "It took me a week to get it just the way I like."

Alexander cleared his throat. "Um, Rip? Nikki?" he said. "I'm sorry about my freak-out yesterday. I just, uh, miss the good old days . . . I'm glad we're hanging out again."

"Me too, Salamander," said Nikki.

"Me three!" said Rip. He slapped Alexander on the back. "Now let's play *Atomic Moon Blasters*! My new computer should be under here somewhere."

Rip tossed laundry aside.

DING! There was a typewriter under the laundry pile.

Rip blinked. "Where did my computer go?!" he shouted.

60

There was a sheet of paper in the typewriter. "What's this?" asked Alexander as he yanked it out. A few crumbs went flying.

THE SWEETEST THINGS ARE OLD-FASHIONED THINGS.

"Ugghhh." Rip groaned. "First, Mom gets on me about eating too many sweets. And now she's leaving me weird notes?"

Alexander looked at his friends. "I don't think Rip's mom left that note," he said. "Crazy stuff is happening here and all over town . . . the billboard, my doorknob, the record player, the telephone, and now this! Not to mention those monster cards! This can only mean one thing: The monsters are back."

"We've been over this, Salamander," said Nikki. "We defeated *all* the monsters."

"She's right," said Rip. "The S.S.M.P. is out of business. So let's just —"

CLUMP-CLOMP!

The three friends jumped.

"It sounds like something is in your attic," said Alexander.

"Or some*one*," said Nikki. "Like your mom, maybe?"

Rip shook his head. "She's taking a bath."

CLUMP-CLOMP! CLUMP-CLOMP! CLUMP-CLOMP!

The bumps came faster, and louder, matching Alexander's beating heart.

CHAPTER 11

ATTIC ATTACK

CREEEEAK! Alexander crept up the attic stairs behind his two friends. He pointed to the top step. "More crumbs," he whispered.

They walked inside.

The attic was filled with old stuff — furniture, books, paintings, and toys.

"Look at all this junk!" said Rip, opening a birdcage.

CLUMP-CLOMP-CLUMP!

The friends whirled around.

A nearby desk was bumping and lurching as if it were alive.

"That's what we heard before! Something's in there!" said Nikki.

The desk stopped moving.

Alexander stepped forward and opened the rolltop. The only thing inside was a shiny silver tin.

Alexander tapped on the tin. He picked it up.

"Whoa," he said. "Whatever's in here is *really* heavy."

"Like gold coins?" guessed Rip.

Alexander gave it a shake. "It feels solid. Like a brick."

He started to open the tin, when —

PLONK! The tin burst open. A small brownish creature leaped out and smacked into Alexander's shoulder.

Alexander yelped as he fell into a pile of old suitcases.

"The creature's getting away!" shouted Nikki.

The brown blur scrambled up a grandfather clock and dashed along the frame of a huge mirror.

Then it scurried out the door, leaving a trail of crumbs.

CRUSTY CRUD

Rip and Nikki pulled Alexander to his feet.

"Gross!" said Nikki. "What's that on your shoulder?"

Alexander looked in the mirror. There was a blob of sticky glop on his shoulder. A second later, the glop became crusty and hard.

"Is it cement?" asked Nikki.

"Or did you sneeze on yourself?" asked Rip.

"No!" Alexander snapped. "It's monster slime or something! This crud is right where that thing smacked into me. That was clearly a monster!"

"Whatever it was," said Nikki, "it's getting away!"

They raced through the house, following the trail of crumbs. The trail led over a rocking chair, under a piano, around a globe, and ended at a laundry chute.

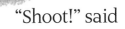

"Shoot!" said Alexander. "We can't fit —"

SLAM! A door slammed below them.

"It's downstairs!" yelled Rip.

They rushed to the first floor. They searched every room, but the crumb trail was gone.

"Do you think that slam we heard could've been the cellar door?" asked Nikki.

"Impossible!" said Rip. "That door has been locked since we moved in."

"Maybe it was the front door," said Alexander. "The monster could have gone outside."

They all looked at the front door of the house — and gasped. Through the stained-glass window, they saw a tall, looming figure, dressed in red.

BAM-BAM-BAM!

The figure pounded at the door.

CHAPTER 13

IN THE WEEDS

Rip had his hand on the doorknob. Alexander and Nikki stood back.

"Open it on three," said Alexander. "One —"

Rip threw open the front door.

"Somebody ordered a pizza?" asked the man standing outside.

The three friends stared at the pizza guy.

"Perfect timing!" said Rip's mom. She came downstairs and paid for the pizza.

Then they all had a picnic on the living room floor. Alexander nibbled at his pizza slice, peering out the window for signs of the attic monster.

Finally, Ms. Bonkowski headed to the kitchen with their dirty plates.

"We need to search outside," Alexander whispered.

"Good call," said Rip. He shouted down the hallway. "Hey, Mom! Can we go play flashlight tag outside?"

"Sure," Ms. Bonkowski called from the kitchen. "But it's past my bedtime! I'll see you kids at breakfast."

"Thanks, Mom!" Rip shouted.

The three friends headed out into the moonlight. For an hour, they searched the high weeds in the front yard. There was no sign of the monster.

"We've lost its trail. Not even a single crumb!" said Nikki. "Let's check The Brambles."

They walked around to the backyard. Rip swung his flashlight over to the thorn maze. White figures glowed like frozen ghosts.

"Those statues creep me out," said Alexander.

THE BRAMBLES

Alexander sniffed the air. "Do you guys smell something?"

"It smells sweet," said Rip. "Like donuts!"

"It's coming from your kitchen," said Nikki. "Look — the light's on!"

They crept over and crouched outside the back door.

CLANK! SPLASH! BONK!

"Someone is clanging pots and pans around," said Alexander.

"It must be the grocery bandit!" said Rip.

Nikki rolled her eyes. "Or your mom."

Rip stood up and grabbed the doorknob.

"Rip, no!" said Alexander.

"Gotcha!" Rip shouted as he barged into the kitchen. Alexander and Nikki stumbled in after him.

"NO!" growled a voice from inside. "I got *you*!"

PIECE OF CAKE

The kitchen was warm and smelled really sweet. A huge pot bubbled on the stove. But there was nobody else in the room.

"Where did that voice come from?" asked Alexander, turning off the stove.

He looked down and gulped. Two shiny red eyes peered out from the oven.

"That looks like . . . a monster," said Rip.

"Salamander was right!" said Nikki. "We *didn't* stop all the monsters!"

"You got most of us," grumbled the voice. "But not little old me!"

Alexander picked up a rolling pin. Nikki grabbed a spatula. Rip balled up his fists. They took a step toward the oven.

"For years, I've been waiting for my chance to strike," said the voice. "When a new square-headed monster moved into MY house, I knew the time was right."

FWOOM! The oven door flew open, filling the room with heat.

BLOMP! A loaf-shaped cake flopped onto the floor. It was bumpy, brown, and covered with shiny bits of fruit and nuts.

"Is that a . . . ?" said Nikki.

"Fruitcake?" said Alexander.

"NO!" said the monster. "I am a BRUTE-CAKE! I'm eighty times tougher than a regular fruitcake."

"Ha!" said Rip. "You?! You're so tiny!"

The brute-cake's glazed eyes stared at Rip. "Not in this heat," it said. "Watch me RISE!"

The cake swelled up until it was the size of a baby elephant. Then — **WHAM!** — it socked Rip in the jaw with a nut-covered fist.

The brute-cake turned to Alexander and Nikki next. "You want a piece of me?!"

The cake sprang at them.

GLORP! Nikki jabbed the brute-cake with her spatula. Crumbs flew everywhere.

"Those crumbs we keep finding — they came from you!" she said.

HURFF! The cake shoved Nikki into Alexander and Rip. They stumbled backward into a rack of pots and pans.

"You'll never beat us, nut loaf!" yelled Rip.

"I don't want to *beat* you!" said the brute-cake. "I want to collect you — well, two of you!"

"Collect us?" asked Nikki, hopping to her feet.

"Yes. I collect monsters!" said the cake. "That is why I changed the grocery list, so I could cook up a batch of my special icing!"

The crusty crud on my shirt must be icing! thought Alexander.

The cake stomped over to the stove and tasted a spoonful of drippy white glaze.

"Perfect," said the brute-cake. The monster lifted the pot of glaze, and — **GOOSH!** — dumped it all over itself.

Then the brute-cake pointed a dripping finger at Nikki.

She charged at the cake with her spatula. **SPLAWTCH!** The monster blasted Nikki with a gush of warm glaze.

Instantly, she became a shiny white statue.

CHAPTER 15

THE CELLAR

Alexander scrambled over to Nikki. "What have you done to her?!" he yelled.

"She's perfectly preserved in monster glaze!" said the brute-cake.

"That does it!" Rip shouted. "I'm gonna clobber this cobbler. Monster to monster!" He picked up a large cake crumb and took a bite.

GRAAWRRR!! Rip transformed into Monster-Rip: the knuckle-fisted punch-smasher.

The brute-cake raised its lumpy arms
and tackled Monster-Rip.

KER-PLANCH! Both monsters
crashed through the locked
cellar door and tumbled
down the stairs.

Alexander ran after them.

The cellar was filled with shiny white statues.
Some were giant. Some were knee-high. They all
had fangs, or claws, or wings, or tails.

The brute-cake's monster collection is HUGE!
thought Alexander.

In the middle of the statues, Monster-Rip
and the brute-cake circled each other like sumo
wrestlers.

PLAM! Rip swung a punch at the brute-cake. Giant crumbs went flying.

The monster yanked an enormous candied walnut from its own gut.

WHOOM! It chucked the nut at Rip.

KER-PLUMMEL! Monster-Rip flew backward, slamming into the wall.

A few ants crawled from Rip's pocket and nibbled on the sweet nut.

BA-DINK! The ants became gi-norm-ants and pushed Monster-Rip back to his feet.

Monster-Rip blinked. He growled.

He looked angry, but dizzy.

The brute-cake pointed
a crusty finger at Rip.

SPLAWTCH! Rip and his
ants instantly froze into a statue.

"Sweet!" said the brute-cake.
"More monsters for my collection!"

"Noooooo!" Alexander yelled.
He charged at the monster. And —

WHOOP! He tripped on
the walnut and landed on
his back.

HUR-HUR-HUR-SNURT-HUR-HUR! The brute-cake
leaned over Alexander, snort-laughing crumbs
into his face. "I don't glaze
kids — only monsters! So
I'm going to crush you the
old-fashioned way!"

The brute-cake jumped
in the air, directly above
Alexander.

A CRUMMY ENDING

As the monster came down, Alexander rolled sideways.

WHAM! The brute-cake landed hard, shaking the cellar. Huge crumbs fell aside.

The monster grunted and hopped to its feet. One of its cranberry eyes was on the floor.

Alexander scurried beneath a statue.

I've seen this monster before, he thought. *On the card I found at the library!*

The brute-cake felt around for its missing eye. "I remember how great Stermont used to be, before the S.S.M.P. was around."

Alexander stood up, careful to stay hidden behind the pickle.

The brute-cake went on. "I heard what you said in Rip's bedroom, Alexander. You're right. Things were better in the old days. We both hate how everything has changed!"

"That's why I've been making improvements around town," the monster continued. "The billboard, the record player, the typewriter, even your doorknob. Once I finish fixing everything up, I will set my monsters free to take over the all-new old-timey Stermont!"

Alexander stepped out from behind the statue and faced the brute-cake. "I see that your collection includes the drill-pickle from your monster cards!"

"The drill-pickle was a great find!" the brute-cake replied. The monster scratched its crumbly head. "But I don't know anything about monster cards. Another monster must have left those to mess with you. Ah — here we go!"

BLORP! The monster popped its eye back in. "*Now* I'll flatten you like gingerbread!"

SNURRRT! The brute-cake snorted like a bull and charged straight for Alexander.

Alexander dove aside at the last second.

The giant cake rammed into the drill-pickle's pointy drill and —

PLOMPFF!

The monster crumbled to pieces.

Suddenly, **CRICKLE-CRACKLE-CRUNCH!** Cracks appeared on the Monster-Rip statue. The white glaze broke apart like an eggshell. Regular-Rip stumbled out.

"Salamander!" Rip said. "As soon as you beat the brute-cake, its glaze crumbled!"

A moment later, Nikki staggered down the steps, covered in glaze bits.

CRICKLE-CRACKLE-CRUNCH! Cracks appeared on all the glazed monsters in the cellar.

"Uh-oh," said Alexander. "Hide!"

The three friends ducked behind some pipes.

CRICKLE-CRACKLE-CRUCKLE-CRACK-CRACKLE-CRUNCH!

"It sounds like fireworks!" Rip shouted.

Every monster in the cellar broke free from its shell. Then —

VWWIIRRRRRRR!! The drill-pickle tunneled through the cellar wall.

Silently, the three friends watched a flood of monsters follow the pickle out into Stermont.

"How many monsters just escaped?" asked Nikki as they headed upstairs.

"A ton!" said Rip. "Plus all the statues outside!"

Alexander yawned as he unrolled his sleeping bag. "If we're going to fight new monsters, we should rest up."

"Hey, look!" said Nikki. "There's something on your pillow!"

"Another monster card!" said Rip.

"We've got to find out who's been leaving these for us!" said Alexander.

He picked up the card.

BRUTE-CAKE

LEVEL 1

The fruity, nutty gift that nobody wants.

| ATTACKS | GLAZE GUSH! | 5 | CAKE POUND! | 10 |

HABITAT

Tin in the attic.

DIET

Candied fruit and nuts.

TYPE

 FOOD

 UNKNOWN

Fruitcake: Never goes bad.
Brute-cake: Started out bad.

© H.S. INDUSTRIES

"Looks like the S.S.M.P. is back in business!" said Alexander. "Everything may be different now. But maybe that's not such a bad thing."

"We don't have a headquarters," said Nikki. "Or any monster-fighting gear."

"You're right. But we do have a new monster notebook — I mean, binder!" said Alexander. "And the important stuff hasn't changed a bit." He looked at his best friends.

Rip yawned. "We'll get started first thing tomorrow. After breakfast, I mean."

The tired monster fighters wriggled into their sleeping bags.

"Good night, you two," said Alexander.

He added the brute-cake card to his S.S.M.P. binder. Then he took out his marker and added a single word.

ABOUT THE AUTHOR

NEW YORK TIMES BESTSELLING AUTHOR
TROY CUMMINGS
LEVEL 0

spent his whole life writing, illustrating, and trying to avoid fruitcake.

ATTACKS HALF-BAKED PUNS **88** OVERCOOKED GAGS **451**

HABITAT
A quiet, sunny office above a loud, dark coffee shop.

DIET
Cupcakes. Cheesecake. Pancakes. ANYTHING but fruitcake!

© H.S. INDUSTRIES

Troy Cummings has no tail, no wings, no fangs, no claws, and only one head. As a kid, he believed that monsters might really exist. Today, he's sure of it.

The idea for the BRUTE-CAKE hit Mr. Cummings like a ton of bricks — or rather, one dense brick — when a librarian friend sent him a fruitcake in the mail. ($9 postage!)

Mr. Cummings has written and/or illustrated more than thirty books, including THE NOTEBOOK OF DOOM series.

THE BINDER OF DOOM
BRUTE-CAKE
QUESTIONS & ACTIVITIES

There are **two** different clubs called the S.S.M.P.: the Super Secret Monster Patrol, and the Stermont Summer Maker Program. Compare and contrast the two clubs. Who are their members? What are their activities?

Alexander's best friends Nikki and Rip are monsters. What kind of monsters are they? Look back at pages 20 and 36 - 37.

Reread page 67. **Chute** and **shoot** are homophones. These words sound the same, but are spelled differently and have different meanings. What are the meanings of **chute** and **shoot**?

The brute-cake likes old-fashioned things, like typewriters. Can you find **three** other old-fashioned things in this story that the monster likes?

Rip's basement was full of glazed monsters. What happens to these monsters at the end of the story? What will the S.S.M.P. do next? Draw and write your own prediction.